Bred by magic

Diana Marie DuBois

Tonya,

Athena

Bred by magic

Diana Marie DuBois

Dogs are bred for our love.

Diana M DuBois

Published by Three Danes Publishing L.L.C.

Cover art by Anya Kelleye
http://www.anyakelleye.com/
Cover photo taken by Diana Marie DuBois
Edited by Maxine Horton Bringenberg
Guardian logo created by P and N Graphics

Acknowledgements and Thank You

~To the three most beautiful Great Danes, for letting me watch you and wanting the attention you so greatly deserve while I wrote.

~I want to extend a big thank you to my Beta Readers. I'm sorry I made y'all cry, but I'm glad you enjoyed this book as much as I did writing it. Thank you Carol, Charlene, Debb, and Cat.

~To Nicole Hicks, thank you for suggesting this short story idea. You are one of my best sounding boards and I am thankful for our messages back and forth.

~My editor, the fabulous Maxine Bridgenberg. Thank you always for everything you do in polishing and tightening my stories.

~Anya Kelley (Onion) once again you designed a beautiful cover. You put so much thought and work into a gorgeous piece of artwork. Thank you for bringing my story of Athena to life and for immortalizing my Lily forever.

~An extended thank you to my big sister, Rhonda Plumhoff, I love you; you were always there for me telling me I could do this.

~If it wasn't for my parents and their continuous support I don't know if I would be where I am today.

~My street team and my fans, oh where would I be without all of y'all.

~Ava, my woodstick. You have no idea how much your belief in me keeps me going. I love you to infinity and beyond.

~Charlotte, thank you for believing in me.

~Lindsey Hines, thank you for putting up with me and encouraging me every day.
~And finally without Barbra Annino a great author and fellow Great Dane lover, I would not have been able to put my own spin on my own stories and bring the spirit of my own Danes into my writing. After reading your books I knew we were kindred spirits with Danes.

Dedication

To Lily who inspired Athena and the Guardians. A fur baby to never be forgotten even though you've crossed over the rainbow bridge. You will forever remain in my heart. Thanks for sharing your life with me. Rest in peace 2005-2014

Note to Reader

When building my world for Voodoo Vows, I wanted something different then a cat to be a companion for Rosie. Being a Great Dane owner I knew I wanted to put this magnificent giant dog into a story. But I also didn't want to make it a familiar even though I was pairing the dog with a witch. With the dog's stature and breading, I was able to create a power to be rivaled. So in there lies how the Guardians were created or bred. I mixed in some magic, drew from history of the breed, and created something I hope you enjoy reading about.

Glossary

Alchemist-a person who has the ability to create the elixir of life, which would confer youth and longevity.
Aura-The essence of a human or magical creature.
Bond-a telepathic connection shared with little one and Alexander.
Bug with blue wings-butterfly.
Big opening with warmth-fireplace.
Copper smell-blood.
Gold lined black box- coffin.
Guardians- a female Great Dane bred with magic to heighten the senses and invoked with magical powers. Always destined to protect a female witch.
Ja- the funny way Alexander said yes
Little one-the nickname the pup had until she received her true name.
Loud metal box-airplane.
Long meat in fluffy bread-lucky dog, hot dog sold in and around Jackson Square.
Magic-substance infused into the guardians and warriors blood.
Round shiny ball-crystal ball.
Parlor tricks-the nonessential tricks alexander taught little one.
Potions-The magic that Alexander and Karl used to create the Guardians and Warriors.
Scribe-a person who trains the puppies and gets them ready for their witch, who will do the rest of their training.

See through people-ghosts.
Silver object-the flask, Alexander drank a magical elixir from. This is what made him never age.
Something sharp-needle to draw blood from the pups to make sure the magic had infused into their bloodstream.
Teardrop object-an amulet with a tear drop from the pup's mother made from the deepest of love, a mother's.
Thin white rag-handkerchief. Usually Karl always had one and he pulled it from his pocket.
Tug-a-war-a game enjoyed by the pups.
Warriors-same as a Guardian except it goes to a male witch and is always a male Great Dane.
Weird creature with big feet-frog.

Table of Contents

“It is important to remember that we all have magic inside us.”

J K Rowling

Magic alive, magic ahead.
Lined in the pages about to be read
Take in the Tale, let the magic spread.
With the wonderful story of how Magic was Bred

born

1658

At the reassuring thump, thump of my mother's heartbeat and the warm protection of her body, I stirred. Hunger ravaged my tummy as I wriggled around until I found her milk. Even more ravenous at each suck, the moment the warm substance flowed through me, my tummy no longer growled. With my swollen belly full to the brim, I rolled over on my side and stretched, then crawled over to a vacant spot and fell fast asleep.

When I woke I wore a warm blanket of my siblings. I kicked my back legs and shuffled my body around until I no longer had a pup on me. Even though my eyes and ears were devoid of the outside world, an overpowering mystical magic whirled in the room.

I crawled to my mother. *Mommy, what's that noise?*

Oh, dear, that's the voices of Alexander and Karl discussing the future of this litter. You know, if you snuggle closer to me you may be able to make out more of what they are saying.

At her prodding I nestled closer to her, and the softness of her fur bristled along my body. With my head against her, I heard their voices vibrate off her. As I listened to the two men, my brothers and sisters scooted in closer, pushing me further up next to my mother's warm body. Her fur tickled my nose as I leaned in.

"Alexander, it looks like we have a good litter this time. We have two females and four males. I think we can find good homes for the males, where they can become great warriors for their warlocks. The females will find good homes with witches they will guard. Yes, this litter is made of excellent stock," the man said softly.

"Ja. I agree Karl." Alexander's thick Danish accent was heavier than normal in his excitement. "I see lots of promise in this litter. I hope this one goes better than the last. But, before we get ahead of ourselves, let's see how many make it through the transition. We need to make sure the magic infused into their bloodstream works well with the potion we will give them after they are a few weeks old. Oh, don't forget to get the amulets ready for the tear drops."

"Yes, sire," Karl said, and hurried from the room.

After I listened to the two men speak of our future and what a great one it was to be, I closed my eyes and fell asleep.

Weeks later

I padded around on my stumpy little legs in the enormous room we inhabited and planned an exciting adventure. The floor underneath my paws felt cold as I stumbled around and tried to get my bearings. I was not sure what this room was, but the sights and sounds were foreign and at the same time exhilarating.

On any given day the room sparkled with an array of colors or objects. The two men would come in and place items on the table in the corner of the room. I could now hear loud, high pitched, and quieter sounds.

Once we had been weaned from our mother we were allowed to explore the large expansive place. Even though I had learned to walk, my legs were sometimes unsteady. The practice was fun, though, especially when I stumbled into my sister and brothers and sent them flying across the room.

One day on my journey across the room, a loud yip came from behind me. All of a sudden, I flipped head-over-bottom and found myself on my back. I stared up at the culprit while he stood over me and dragged his wet slobbery tongue over my face. Before I knew what happened, he pulled his lips back in a menacing smirk, growled, and bit down hard on my ear. I braced my stubby little legs, pushed with all my might, and sent the annoying puppy tumbling across the floor in the opposite direction.

He stood back up, crouched low, and stalked slowly towards me, then growled and made a mad dash in my direction. This time I stood my ground and pounced on him with gusto right before he had the chance to jump. I knocked him on his back and stood over him with my floppy ears in his face and my nose inches away. I pulled my lips back and pretended to growl angrily at him.

We played and scrambled back and forth for hours, to see who would be the first to overthrow the other. When we had played to exhaustion, we bounded over to our mother and curled up next to her and our other littermates.

I awoke in a groggy haze to the sound of a man's voice. "Come, let's get started and mix the two potions, and see how this litter will take this second round of magic."

A sudden curiosity seized me; I stood up and waddled over to the two men. One paw in front of the other, I completed my trek across the room and flopped down next to the man's shoe.

Laughter rang out. "Hahaha. Look Alexander, it seems like we have our first volunteer." The very young man acknowledged me to the red haired man.

The man called Alexander chuckled, picked me up, flipped me around, and inspected every inch of my small body. As he held me in the air, my legs dangled and I wiggled in his grasp. When his face got closer to me, his whiskers above his lip tickled my nose. I reached out my tongue and licked his face in one quick swipe. He laughed and patted me on the head. "Ja, Karl, this one is a female...she will do fine, and look at these odd markings. The spots interspersed with her coloring are quite unique. Which, if I recall, is a sign of prominence. If memory serves me there has been one other dog in history with these markings, and you know she is still a great Guardian." He looked toward Karl before he turned his attention back to me. "You are intended for someone important, little one."

He placed me in his lap and the bumpy material of his robe beneath me massaged my belly. His sympathetic touch seemed to engulf my body, and the golden flecks in his emerald eyes bounced off the candle light while he held me.

The man's eyes glazed over and I wondered what had made him so distraught and caused the suffering I felt coming from him in waves. Karl hoisted himself up from where he sat in a wooden chair across from Alexander. He walked around the table and rested a comforting and reassuring hand on the man's shoulder. "You know we all miss her, but the situation could not be helped. Your wife's injuries were too critical. Persephone did her job guarding her, but the fire had caused too much damage to Dahlia's lungs. And you know if we had not created the Guardians, we would not have had Persephone, and your wife would have died a far more devastating death." I nuzzled into his chest detecting a sadness overcome him.

"I know Karl, and I thank every day the light shines upon us she saved her from that burning pile of rubble."

He looked down at me and scratched behind my ears, his voice soft as he spoke. "That is why I've dedicated my life to creating Guardians, like you little one, to help protect magic and their witches." I nuzzled even closer to him and sensed a calming surround him.

The younger man patted him on the shoulder. "All right, let us get this batch made. It needs time to sit, infuse, and rise to the proper temperature." Karl spoke while he prepared the array of glass bottles along with the ingredients.

My eyes darted back and forth between the two men. But, my curiosity got the better of me as I watched every movement in earnest while they began to mix the potions. One poured a blue liquid into a bottle and then the other poured a pink liquid. When they mixed, the colors turned a bright color of purple. When they were done there were a dozen bottles of different colors and shapes. My eyes were wide and transfixed at what lay before me. The liquid turned foggy and swirled around in the bottles. A white fog puffed up from the top, swirled around, and drifted down to cover the table. I had never seen so many shades of the rainbow, or smelled so many sweet and intoxicating scents. Soon the white clouds of mist dissipated right before my eyes. The aromas surrounding me were heavenly, and even with no idea what they were I wanted to taste them.

My mouth watered the instant the thought popped into my head. I had to have a better look. I stood up in Alexander's lap and placed my front paws on the edge of the table. The more they mixed, the more curious I became. I tried to hoist the back end of my body onto the table. I pushed and pushed with exuberance until my back end dangled between the lap and the hunger inducing mixtures in front of me.

Almost there, I thought. My back paws scrambled in the air to reach the table.

"Oh, no you don't, little one." His gentle laugh subdued me and I felt him pull me back onto his lap. "These are very *important* potions for you and your littermates, and cannot be spilled." He cuddled me to his chest, where I soon fell fast asleep.

Bottles clinking and the wafting smell of smoke woke me. From behind his strong arms that held me, I peeked my head out and witnessed the two still busily working on the potions. This time I noticed a straight line of bottles, and clear teardrop stones, enough for my brothers and sister and I. But all of a sudden a familiar scent drifted over and made my stomach growl.

With my nose in the air I caught the scent of beef, and my nose twitched with eagerness in the direction of the smell. Metal bowls slid and clattered around on the floor. I watched as food splattered and flew on the floor, which made me struggle to get out of Alexander's hold, but he gripped me even tighter than before. "Not yet. You must take this before you eat."

I cocked my head at him, hungry and eager to do whatever he wanted in order to get to the scents that made my belly ache with hunger. He held a glass tube with a pointed opening out to me, and with his other hand squeezed my jaws open, allowing a few wet drops from the tube to fall into my opened mouth. It tasted funny but not bad. I licked my lips and looked up at him, waiting to be told that food was next.

"Sure thing, little one." He put me down and my toenails scratched at the floor trying to get to the scrumptious smell, as I ran to the bowls strewn all about. As I ran I tumbled into one of the bowls and it spun around on the floor before flipping over. Food flew in the air and landed on the floor. As I gobbled it up a clump fell on my back. I scanned the room to see if anyone had noticed, but my littermates were too busy scarfing down their own food. After I finished and my tummy was swollen and full, I decided to take another nap.

I woke next to my playmate from earlier. His head rested on my foot so I nudged him with the other one, but he didn't move. This time I stretched out my leg and kicked him hard and he moved off my foot.

After a few moments he looked up at me wide eyed. *Do you want to play*? Before I could answer he pounced. We played and tumbled some more and ran here and there, and with every move we got more used to our legs. After a good game of tug o' war with an old rag we'd found abandoned in the room, my brother and I once again found ourselves drained.

When I awoke later, my stomach fluttered with an indescribable strange feeling. It flowed like ripples through my entire body and fear encased me. Panic ensued, and I looked for my brother. I found him sprawled on his back with his legs in the air, snoring, which seemed to be his favorite position to sleep in. He seemed very content in his dream state, and he kicked his legs in the air.

Brother, wake up. I shoved him with my paw. When he didn't move I bit his ear. He cracked one eye open and closed it again with a huff. *Wake up! I feel odd.*

He rolled over and looked up at me with his tongue hanging out of the corner of his mouth. *Oh, there is nothing wrong with you. The magic is taking over and mixing in your body. I had the same feeling, it'll pass.* And like that he rolled back over and continued to snore.

I barked, nudged him once more, and tackled him. *What do you mean, magic?* I asked with a growl.

He rolled over halfway on his side, cocked his head at me with one eye opened, and looked at me. *I heard the two men say we are all born for a reason...some to guard, some to become warriors.*

*Oh...*I replied.

At the reassurance from my brother, I sat on my haunches and licked my paw, wondering which I was supposed to be, when a loud commotion alerted us to a problem.

"Alexander! Oh, Alexander, we have a distressing issue, sire," Karl yelled, and ran through the room, his voice echoing off the walls. I could see a small limp form held carefully and quite still in his hands despite how Karl's body jiggled in his haste. Two black ears fell over his arm. I howled out in fear. Could it be? Was this one of my siblings?

Alexander got up from his chair, sighed heavily, and hung his head, "I wonder if the potion..."

Karl interrupted him. "No. I think this one had been sick. The potion worked fine; there seems to be an abnormality in its body that worked against the potion. Look, the others are doing fine and grow a little more each day. Once they find their new homes, they'll be of great stature and power."

I became curious and tilted my head in the two men's direction, trying to understand what they meant and keep my eyes on the limp body now in Alexander's arms. He stroked the soft fur, and I saw the pain in his eyes from losing the puppy. My other littermates came over to where we sat, their heads hung low. *We have lost our sister.* They cried in unison. *What if we are next?*

No. It can't be. We are strong. I stuck out my paw and it landed on the floor in the middle of the puppies standing around. I tried my best to comfort them, but they all began to talk at once and a ferocious pain pounded in my head.

No...we will be fine and we ***will*** *find our place in this world.* I stood tall and proud at my words.

My brother came up behind me then stood to my left. *Our sister is right. We are strong, and we will survive and move on to guard and become the best warriors the magical world will ever know.*

The young man glanced at us when our incessant barking began. “Sire, what has gotten into them?”

“They sense the loss of one of their own, but they’ll calm down soon.” He looked over in our general direction.

“How do you know?”

The tall red-haired man looked my way and replied, after winking at me, “I just know. Now, let’s take care of this little one and let her brothers and sisters mourn.” He glanced back at the man and I knew in an instant he could hear me, if not all of us. His power began to emanate from him, the lights flickered, and it felt like an electric current sparked throughout the room.

I turned back towards my littermates and saw they had been somewhat soothed by my words.

After Alexander had placed our sister in a box, wrapped in a special blanket, he called to us. “Come on, pups.”

Our steps were slow and concise as we followed the two men solemnly out the door, them carrying the small, brown box. When the two men stopped they positioned it on the ground, surrounded by a pile of dirt. We trudged up to the box that lay on the ground. One by one, we stuck our nose in the box to say goodbye. When my turn came I slowly padded up to the box, stuck my nose in, and sniffed my sister. She looked peaceful, and seemed to be sleeping. I nosed the blanket over her all the way until it covered her, then stepped back as Alexander put the lid on and placed the box gently in the hole. When Karl picked up the shovel leaning against the tree, I cocked my head left to right and felt the urge to help, but I decided to wait. At the last moment my brothers and I stepped up to the covered hole. Each one of us shoved a little bit of the dirt over with our paws and patted it down, similar to what Karl had done with the shovel.

Afterwards we all crawled on top of the dirt. We didn’t care the ground itched our bellies as we lay down; we had to tell our sister goodbye. We all curled into each other, sharing warmth and closeness. I fell asleep to the sounds of soft whimpers, and knew they were still worried about whether they would be next to pass to the other side.

When I woke, the light in the sky had almost gone out. I looked over and saw Alexander standing by a tree. He leaned against it sipping from a silver object. I heard him call to Karl to come get us.

We were taken inside to Alexander's office to be looked over one at a time. He picked me up last. "Come, little one. Let's make sure you have taken well to the magic inside of you." He placed me on a cold metal table that made me shiver. The examination took only a few minutes.

Before I knew it Karl picked me up and held me gently close to his chest. The tall man stuck me with something sharp, and I wiggled from the pain, wanting to get down.

"Hold on little one," Karl said as he patted my head. I settled down and watched a red liquid fill up a tiny bottle. After all the tests were done, he put me back among my siblings to play.

The next day brought promise for us all. I overheard Alexander and Karl talking about how the magic shouldn't take another puppy because they had been successful. The magic had passed through our bloodstream and we should all survive and be ready to go to our new homes, to perform the duties we had been bred for.

One bright warm day my littermates and I were allowed outside to play. The green blades of grass on the ground felt peculiar and itchy under my paws, but the sensation to run took hold of me. Out of the corner of my eye I noticed my brother zigzagging back and forth across the yard. I bounded after him to see what he chased with such excitement. When I caught up him, he had his nose close to the ground and his back end up in the air. His tail wagged hard and made him shake all over. At that moment, I knew he had something cornered.

What is it? I asked.

Not sure, but it is scared of me, he boasted.

I walked around him and caught a glimpse of his prize, a little green fat thing. My brother and this little weird creature with big feet had begun to stare at each other, neither one willing to be the first to move. *Ooh, what is it? Don't let him get away*, I barked at him.

All of a sudden he leapt and caught it in his mouth. *I have it!* His excitement came through, even with the creature sticking out of the corner of his mouth.

Good! Let's take it to Karl, he'll tell us what this thing is! I leapt up and down with excitement.

We trotted off in search of the young man, my brother trying not to crush the thing, while I followed close behind. We found Karl and my brother spat the lifeless thing from his mouth and watched as it dropped to the ground.

"Hey, what is this we have here? Oh, did you two find a frog? Very good, but it seems to be hurt."

I walked over to the frog and nudged it with my nose. It didn't move.

My brother leapt and bounded around the young man's feet as if he had done the most amazing thing ever.

In my opinion, he didn't do anything special. He had it cornered and pounced on it. I could have done that too. I barked, turned around three times, and placed my head down on my paws.

Karl laughed and picked up the frog. "Yes, little one, I am sure you could." Karl rubbed on the little frog in circular motions until it began to stir. I heard it croak and watched Karl put it back on the grass. It hopped off in the opposite direction from us, as fast as its weird legs would carry it.

I crawled over closer to Karl's feet, my back legs sprawled out behind me, and watched my brother run off chasing the frog. *I hope he doesn't hurt it again.*

"Don't worry, he won't, little one. The frog will tease him, but your brother won't be able to catch him again." He gave a short laugh and a soft, subtle cough.

After a few hours of watching my littermates play, I decided to go back inside and find Alexander. I struggled up the back steps, tumbling twice. Once I made it to the top I bounded into the castle and scrambled around the corner into his cluttered laboratory, where my mother lay by his feet. I snuggled up next to her and fell asleep, but not before my siblings padded in to pile around us.

bonding and goodbyes

With time I became close to Alexander and knew I held a special place in his heart. Not that he didn't care for the others, but since the first moment he had held me in his arms we'd formed a bond, and I never noticed him talking to the rest like he did with me. I learned quite a bit from him, from his stories about his hopes and dreams, and the possibilities he saw for the future.

When the others slept, he would often pick me up and we would have long conversations. Many of our talks took place through our mental bond. Instead of barking my responses as I did to Karl or Cook, he talked in my head and I responded in the same way.

Through the years, one by one, my littermates left to go to their new homes. Our mother witnessed every goodbye, her eyes saddened by the possibility she might never see them again. After I told them goodbye and wished them a good life, I moved to stand back in the shadows.

My mother and the rest of the staff would say their goodbyes, and each pup received a gift.

The day my closest friend, and brother, left to go to his new home, I became withdrawn and sullen.

Don't be sad, sister. He nudged me with his paw and nuzzled my face.

I'm trying, but I'm afraid I'll never go to my new home or find my witch, I whined.

Little sister, you will find your home and witch, and you'll be great. Trust me, I know what I say to be the truth. I also know we'll see each other again one day. He nuzzled me once more and ran to the door, ready for his new life.

I whimpered when I realized I stood in the empty great hall of the castle all alone. Thoughts flooded my head that soon he would have a name and be loved by those he would fight for. He wouldn't become a Guardian like me, but he would be as important. He would serve a powerful warlock. And, if it came down to it, he would be sent to war to fight for those he swore to protect.

I walked up to Alexander head down, and a small whine came out; he picked me up. "No worries, little one; your time will come…I promise. I have it on great authority your fate is a wonderful one, and the one you will guard will be an important and loving witch." The honesty flowing from him eased my pain and heartache.

"Though it will not be an easy journey, you and your witch will be there for each other."

I looked up at my friend and confidant, and knew no truer words had ever been spoken. He laughed at my expression as I cocked my head; I licked his face and wagged my tail as joy once again filled me.

friends and death

Over the course of the following years, I became much closer to Alexander and Karl. I hadn't grown much since I hadn't been placed with my witch yet, but I had grown some. Allowed free roam of the grounds and castle, I made the place my own. Any of the household staff could find me in the kitchen when Cook prepared the food. When I entered she always offered me a treat, making it one of my favorite places to visit.

One day when the light in the sky began to change to yellow, orange, and pink, I went on a long walk with Karl in the gardens. Soon I found a mouse hiding under a bush and chased it out of its spot. I ran back and forth following the little brown creature, though I made sure to never hurt it; I had learned a lesson with the frog. The small creatures needed to be cared for, not hurt. Even though my brother didn't mean to harm him, I was glad the frog lived longer. It was a memory I held close to me every day.

We would have long conversations; though I didn't have the telepathic link with Karl like I did with Alexander, he still managed to understand me. Once we got back to the castle, I would always run straight to Alexander. I didn't know what it was, but I felt a comforting presence being near him.

One day Karl noticed the interaction between the two of us, and took Alexander aside. "You know, Alexander, if I didn't know better I would swear you are bonding with that dog."

He laughed and stood while he crossed his arms over his chest. "I know, Karl. But I feel she is a special one, and I want to train her well. I know she is destined for greatness."

Alexander reached down and petted me.

"Sire, you do not plan on training her yourself? You know that is the job of her witch." Karl's jaw actually dropped open.

"Ja, I do. As you said, she has been here the longest, she will need to be trained, and I did a pretty damn good job with her mother."

"You must be careful, sire. She *must* know she will leave this place one day. I'm concerned for your well-being also; you, like her, must be prepared for her to leave. She's the one who has stayed in the castle the longest," Karl warned him.

"I know, my old friend, I know. I will be careful, and trust this when I say I am prepared to let her go when it is time. I am proud of her and

I want to be a part of her being the best Guardian. And deep down she knows and feels the bond, and knows it will not last once she meets her witch," Alexander told his scribe.

Karl shook his head, his glasses on the edge of his nose. With his thumb and forefinger he removed them and pulled a thin white rag from his pocket. He shook it out and wiped his glasses, then replaced them on his face and looked at Alexander over the rims. "But remember, she is not yours, and will, in time, find her place in this world. And I will not always be here for you to lean on."

Before he left, he knelt down and faced me. He reached out a hand and his touch on my head comforted me like warm sunshine, and he whispered to me, "You *do* remind him of your mother." My tail wagged and my entire body shook. When I raised my paw, he shook it and laughed. "Alexander, please tell me you have not been teaching her parlor tricks." Karl turned and walked off towards his room; he shook his head and laughed at the master of the house.

On our next walk I noticed Karl made strange noises. It sounded similar to one my brother did when he hacked up a piece of meat he didn't like. But, somehow, I knew this noise wasn't good. He coughed into a thin, white rag, which turned redder with each use. A copper smell stung my nose. With a hurried movement he tried to hide the cloth in his pocket, but I still caught a glimpse of it. When we came home that day, I ran to my friend to relay what I had seen with Karl.

I ran in barking with worry. The tall red-haired man I knew to be my closest friend sat in a chair. His arm dangled limply over the side. I quickened my pace towards him and with care I nuzzled his hand with my head. *Alexander, there is something wrong with Karl.*

"I know little one, I know. Karl is sick. He has what's called tuberculosis. I know you don't understand what that entails, but I know you can sense my pain." His voice was laced with tons of pain and hurt at the mere thought of the loss of a friend he knew he had no control over.

I whimpered when his pain blossomed into every fiber of my body. The hair prickled along my spine and the sensation he had done this to me surged through my body. I tried with everything I had to shake the intense heartache, but it remained. I knew my training had officially begun. He had filled me with all of his pain and misery. Once he stopped, I left Alexander to his suffering for his friend and made my way through the halls of the castle. I turned a corner and headed through the open door to the kitchen. I went in search of Cook, to see if she had some scraps left over.

She greeted me with a small smile, her plump round body moving smoothly around the kitchen. "Hello, pup. Are you here for a snack?" Sadness filled her voice as she spoke to me.

I barked, *yes*, and though she couldn't understand my words she walked over to the stove. She pulled some meat from a pot and poured it into my food bowl after she filled it. My ears perked up and I eavesdropped on her conversation with the other staff, paying close attention to their whispers.

"You know it's because he refuses to take the elixir Master Alexander offered him. But, he always said he intended to die like a man." Cook lowered her voice. "I don't understand why Karl won't accept the gift offered to him."

Once done with my dinner I made my way to the room I'd spent many a night in. Before I could make it, I heard a noise coming from the room next door. I snuck over, tried not to make a sound, and peeked around the corner into the room. Karl lay in his bed, a strange smell coming from the room.

"Is that you, little one?" His voice was faint and raspy.

Woof, woof, I barked.

"Come here."

I crept from around the door and walked towards him. With both paws placed on the bed, I wiggled and grunted until I had made it all the way up beside him. I lay down by the old man, and could feel his pain and sadness. I placed my head on his chest and hoped it would be enough to calm the ache. I felt a weak hand begin to pet me.

"Listen to me closely. Alexander is correct...you are very special. Please, my young friend, take care of him until you're connected with your witch. He'll need you when I am gone. The man is stubborn, and won't admit it, but he will need another scribe. He will need someone like me who will care for him."

I'll do my best. I burrowed my head under his arm.

"Little one, you offer me the kindest of comfort, and I thank you for your gift. Your witch will be a lucky one to have you...and I promise, she is worth the wait." His weak whisper gave me hope and broke my heart all at the same time. I stayed there with him until he fell asleep and his breathing settled.

In the following weeks, our walks became fewer and fewer, but I would always go to his room and lay beside him. He became weaker and could no longer pet me for very long, but I always stayed with him until sleep claimed him. When the servants brought his food, they were instructed to bring me mine as well, since I now would not leave his side, except for forced breaks to water the lawn.

The day Karl died the castle went into mourning. I had been ushered out when the doctor came to see him. I sensed it wouldn't be much longer before he would leave us, and I bounded through the house at full force. I had to make it in time to tell him goodbye. My paws skidded to a halt right outside the door to his room, and I shifted my feet, worried and scared I was too late. I saw a man leave; he carried a black bag and shook his head. Alexander followed behind him closely.

"Come here, little one." I almost didn't recognize the nearly inaudible voice.

I padded over to him and looked into the face of a man I no longer recognized. Alexander had returned and stood behind me.

I turned to Alexander. *He doesn't look so good, does he, Master?*

He shook his head at me and took great care as he lifted me onto the bed. I could hear strange noises coming from elsewhere in the room, but my focus remained on my friend, the one who'd taken long walks with me in the garden. The one who'd spoken to me, even though he couldn't understand my replies. I nudged my head under his hand and stayed there, silently hoping he would get better. When I woke, black cloth hung from every nook and cranny in the room.

The next day, as the household solemnly bustled around the castle, I overheard Cook say a few of the well-known witch families would take Karl to his final resting place. When the witches and warlocks arrived, I recognized a few of the families belonging to my siblings. Hope surfaced at seeing them again, as I wondered if they would show up as well.

All of a sudden, I noticed the warlocks on either side of the magnificent gold lined black box that contained my friend. They hoisted it up and marched outside with heads bowed in reverence. I followed the procession of witches, warlocks, and household staff outside of the castle.

With a heavy heart, I trotted over towards where Alexander stood by himself. I sat down close to him in hopes my presence would soothe him. I looked around for my brothers, but then my attention was turned to a man dressed in black. He stood in front of the box and read from a book. As the man spoke, I lay down and crossed my paws under my head. When they began to lower the box into the ground, I stood up and watched Alexander, his vacant stare focused into the distance. I asked Alexander, *Where are my brothers?* He stayed silent, and I felt even more at a loss. I wanted my family, like the humans had.

I looked around again and caught a glimpse of a young woman. She stood across from us, pulled a cloth from her pocket, and dabbed at tears as they slid free down her cheeks. I looked at the hole and thought I could have dug it for him. I shook my head, pulled it back up, and saw the woman gaze in my direction.

With a ghost of sadness her smile creased her lips, but it somehow comforted me. I wanted to know more about her, but knew it wasn't the time to bother Alexander with such trivial questions. As we headed back toward the castle, I noticed four huge dogs with pointed ears standing on a hill, looking down at the burial site. Their enormous statures towered even from where I stood; their familiarity weighed heavily on my memory.

Three of them turned and began to walk away, but one stood still, and I could tell he stared, not at the humans, but at me. I stared back before I turned and ran back home. The master of the castle needed me, more than I needed to figure out who stood up on the hill.

Once we arrived home, Alexander became even more inconsolable. I didn't know how to help him, so I lay at his feet with my head over my paws. When I chanced a look at him, he motioned me into his lap. I noticed he drank from his silver flask. I knew, from paying close attention to the people of the house when they spoke of Alexander, the flask contained a potion. But, somehow, I knew it contained a different type of potion than the one he had begged Karl to drink. He began to mumble under his breath, but I heard every word.

"He had turned eighteen when he came to work for me. He came from a prominent clan of squires, you know. The older he got, the more we became friends, and I leaned on him for more than his loyalty. I wish he had stayed with me. I feel it will take a lot for me to gain the trust and confidence of another like I held with him."

an old friend

On one particular day, I decided to go and play by myself in the lush garden. The place felt empty without Karl, and the need to get out to run and play overcame me. The flowers were in full bloom and the sweet aroma cascaded throughout the garden. The bugs fluttered and flitted all over. I trotted through the grass and flowers and around the big tree until I found a new friend.

I began to chase the bug with beautiful wings of blue, black, and gold. It landed on my nose, and my eyes crossed as I tried to see it better. Its wings fluttered in a fast motion as I gazed at its beady little eyes. Without any notice it flew off, creating a small whirlwind.

A sudden, familiar scent invaded my nose. I ran around though the trees and slammed to a halt in front of two giant paws. The feeling of awe spread through me while I looked up at the huge dog.

"Hello, little sister." A deep voice laughed and boomed.

The sight of the large dog had me stunned. "Is it really you?" I walked around and under him. The realization I hadn't even touched him as I made my trek caused me excitement, and made me hope I would be big like him one day.

"Yes it is. We have come to the castle to thank the red one and let him know my name." He looked down at me and his jowls hung low.

"But you're so...*huge*. Wait, you have a name?" My question was laced with hurt and sadness.

He dipped his head down to mine and our noses touched. "Yes. My name is Ares. And you, my little sister, will have a name too one day. I know you're tired of waiting, but it *will* happen."

I continued to walk around and inspect every inch of him. His ears stood straight up, unlike mine which were still very floppy and—in my opinion—always in the way. His dark blue, almost greyish, color seemed darker and shinier. His paws were huge and heavy when I tried to move them.

He laughed and lay his huge body down to my level. "How are you holding up?" he asked. "We heard about Karl. I am sorry, little sister. I know how much you treasured your friendship."

I crawled inside the opening of his paws and nuzzled him. "It is okay. We are managing. Alexander took it hard, but I am good. Why didn't you show up? Shouldn't you have been here? I saw all of the witches and warlocks here, but not you."

"We were here but out of sight; trust me, we paid our respects. He had been a part of our lives as much as yours. Don't you remember spotting us? I thought I saw you look our way as we stood on the cliff overlooking the castle."

The memory of the huge dogs above me on the cliff came back in an instant. "Oh, *those* huge dogs that day on the cliff," my voice stammered. "You're telling me that those dogs were my brothers?"

He nodded. "Yes."

I once again became distracted with his size. "I wish I could be big like you right now." He nudged my head up with his paw and I looked at him. "I mean, look at you...your head is gigantic." I laughed and poked him in the nose with my paw.

He chuffed and knocked me over with his paw. "And yours is quite small."

I rolled back over to look at him sideways and noticed a funny shaped object on his collar. It dangled and swung back and forth with his head. I sat up, reached my paw out, and batted at it. The swing of it back and forth was hypnotizing.

"What *is* that?" I asked him, watching the blue teardrop object come to a sudden stop. I had the urge to swat at it again, but before I reached my paw up I stopped, because it looked important.

"This is a special gift from our mother when we leave to go to our new homes," he told me as he looked down at me with his kind grey eyes. I bowed my head in worry I would never get one. "Little sister, you'll get one, don't you worry. Mother made one for each of us when we were born." He looked curious, his eyes filled with concern and love. "How is Mother?"

"She's doing great. She is in Alexander's study if you want to see her before you leave."

"I do, but first I am here to spend some well-deserved time with you."

While Alexander and my brother's people discussed things in the main house, Ares and I continued to catch up. He told me all about the outside world. With every word my excitement built and anxiety hit like a ton of bricks to get out and begin my life. My life right now stood at a standstill.

I stood up and sank down into my attack stance. "Come, brother, for old times' sake." I laughed when he took a boulder sized paw and knocked me over. I rolled over and over and landed in a bush.

"I will do anything for you, little sister." He chuckled while taking his all too familiar stance with me, ready to attack.

Since he had grown big, compared to me, he didn't play rough like when we were both pups.

He rolled me over with his huge paws, and his deep laugh echoed through the yard. I got up and tried to run away from him. He stuck his paw out to grab me, and barely missed me as my feet scooted underneath him. He caught me by the tail with his paw the next time I ran past him. His laughter boomed while I tried to scramble from his hold. When I regained my freedom, I ran and nipped his legs with my sharp puppy teeth. He rid himself of my annoying nipping by moving his leg while I was still latched on. I bounced up in the air and landed a few feet away from him. After we played and chased for a few more minutes, Ares nudged me with his paw.

"I've got to get back home." With his giant head dipped down to my level, he told me, "Sister, I see prominence in your future. And I know for a fact, we'll see each other one day again."

I watched him leave, a little sad but also full of hope. I ran inside in search of Alexander, to tell him how my visit went with my brother.

my training, or parlor tricks

Many months after we lost Karl, Alexander started training me. We worked on paying attention to how my witch would feel and think. I needed to learn to react in a hurry if she happened to be in danger. I had already learned so much from this man. Though he told me I'd been born with magical gifts, he often added I needed to strengthen them.

"Now, little one, you must remember when you meet your witch, even though you have powers, you must only reveal them at the right time. You'll start to grow when you bond with her, and after her powers will sync with yours. But the majority of yours will remain dormant until she grows into hers."

Alexander, how come you didn't train my brothers?

"Oh little one, there are many other scribes who work in the castle."

Aghast, I asked, *there are other scribes? I didn't know we had other scribes.*

He laughed. "No, little one, Karl happened to have been a longtime friend of mine. We all considered him part of us, and well, you could call him the main scribe. But, we do have other scribes we send with the puppies, to watch over them and train them with their new families."

I cocked my head, excited to learn new things, but still confused on why I was left behind when everyone else had found their homes.

He sensed my sadness and spoke comforting words. "The reason is because you're special, but I will fill you in on a little secret. If you had gone sooner, I would have sent Karl with you," he told me, winking and ruffling my fur.

I sprawled out on the floor with my legs behind me. *Will you watch over me when I go to my new home?* I edged closer to get my ears scratched more.

"My job is to make sure you are always safe, and yes, to always keep an eye on you. However, in my vision, I have seen your witch and she needs your help in her craft. She's new and doesn't know what she is...which makes her extra special."

What will you teach me? I asked.

"I will teach you the art of magic, protection, and seeing auras. You are already very powerful; others will come to you that even I have no idea about."

With a tilt of my head I asked, *Magic? I thought I already had magic in me.*

"Ja, but you *must* learn to protect your witch if ever she is in trouble. You have to be able to sniff out those who wish to harm you or your witch. If, for *any* reason, you come across black magic—the darkest of all magic—you'll still be able to help and protect her."

I whined, feelings of fear and worry filling me like a balloon. It sounded like a huge responsibility. And what if one of us got lost?

"Even if you get separated from her, you will always be able to find her. That, however, is another discussion."

We began to practice all the skills needed to learn to protect my witch. In my first lesson I learned how to transform my body.

"Start slow little one, not too fast."

I nodded my head and thought real hard; one ear jerked and moved a little. I tried even harder to change the other ear. With all my might I tried, and my ear flopped and jerked, and suddenly I felt air pass where my ear used to hang by my head. I ran over to the object hung on the wall that reflected my face back to me. I jumped up and down, and with my excitement my ear flopped back down. Sadness enveloped me.

"No worries little one; with more practice your ears will stay up. But remember to do it when you notice your witch's powers grow."

I nodded and bounced back to him. Throughout the day I learned many things, including how to put a small barrier around me. He said my barrier would become bigger and stronger with my size and powers.

Next he taught me what I remembered Karl calling "parlor tricks." So, I learned how to move objects with my thoughts.

"Here, try this." He placed a small bottle on the table, and a feeling of amazement overcame me while I watched the bottle move to the edge of the table and back to the middle.

He nodded his head at me to try. I looked at the bottle and concentrated hard. It didn't move an inch, no matter how hard I focused on it. *Why can't I move it?*

"It takes time, little one," he replied, pushing the thought into my head.

Intent on getting the bottle to move, I concentrated even harder and thought of the object. I focused harder and cleared my head as Alexander instructed. I squinted up my eyes and sent a clear idea to the bottle and *told* it to move. After what felt like an eternity, the bottle wobbled and lurched an inch toward the edge of the table.

I barked with excitement. *I did it! I did it*! I jumped up and down and continued to make noise and sprint around the room in excitement. In my delight, the table the bottle sat on rocked back and forth and tumbled over onto the floor. The loud crash made my ears perk up and alerted me to the mess I'd made. I watched in horror and fear when the bottles crashed and tiny pieces of glass littered the floor like twinkling lights. I ran and slid out of the way and huddled, shaking, by the wall.

A loud laugh echoed off the walls and made me stop and look over to the big man. He held his sides and laughed, hunched over. I walked over to him slowly, with my head down and ears dragging the ground.

"It is okay, little one." He picked me up and my legs dangled in the air. "You did well, and this is only the beginning."

After the lessons, Alexander offered me a bowl of water. "Here. Drink this, it will help you sleep."

I lapped up every bit of the honey flavored water, stretched, and yawned. Drowsiness overpowered me and I trudged off in search of a nice place to sleep. Once asleep, I dreamed of my witch. Her smile filled me with happy thoughts, and I knew our future together would be great. All of a sudden, my dream changed. She seemed to be sad. I tried to chase after her, but my legs refused to move. Her pain and suffering wrapped around me and almost suffocated me, but in an instant, she disappeared. I glanced around and I could no longer see her. An intense fear covered me. There seemed to be something after her, an evil I could sense, but one I knew would test us both.

a new scribe

The day we received our new scribe the household bustled with excitement. A stranger came to the door, and when allowed in, Alexander would have nothing to do with her.

"No!" I could hear him down the hall. "A girl will *never* be my new scribe."

Alexander's loud yells boomed off the walls and scared me, but I trudged on, wanting to see the new human. I trekked through the castle, nervous and excited at the same time. When I turned the corner, I heard her calm reply. "But sire, my father wished it so, and you know it."

"Your father," he yelled, "turned into a fool, and in the end *left* me! He refused my kindness, refused to stay and remain my friend forever." He threw himself down in his chair, filled with anger and hurt.

"Sire, my father loved you like a brother, and you *know* he had plans for us. Which *is* why he refused to stay...and chose to die like a man. You know this to be true." She knelt down and picked his head up to stare into his deep blue eyes. Her hands grazed his hair and she touched her soft lips to his.

What I witnessed made me instantly want to be close to her. Her love and the pink, yellow, and violet colors surrounding her carried me like a breeze towards them. When she noticed me she smiled and turned back towards the red one.

"Is this her? The one my father spoke of?" she asked.

Alexander looked up, and his eyes took on a haunted look with his eyes rimmed in red. "Ja, she is the one he spoke of...."

I had stopped mid step, sat down, and watched them. He called me over and picked me up when I reached him. With my head tilted in her direction, I recognized her as the woman at Karl's burial place.

"Alisa, this is 'little one'." He told her his pet name for me since he could not name me himself. That right had been reserved for our witches and warlocks.

The human called Alisa took me from him and held me up; my legs dangled in the air but almost touched the floor. She held me and I snuggled in her arms. "Oh, Daddy was right. She's absolutely adorable. And she's, *oh*, very strong." She put me down and I crawled into her lap and sniffed her. The sweet flowery mixture of roses and sweet pea permeated the air around me. I snuggled deeper into her, taking the fragrance into my nose. “Alexander, she will definitely be a great Guardian.” She laughed and held me closer.

Without the red one’s approval, Alisa stayed on. I knew deep down he’d be happy once he resigned himself to the knowledge she wouldn’t be going anywhere.

One day while I sat and watched Alexander work, curiosity got the better of me and I wondered why I had never heard of this human who seemed close to Karl. I felt a bit betrayed. “Oh, little one, don’t be upset with him. She had to wait to come to us. When Karl left us, it became her time to return home. You may have seen her at the funeral.” A deep sigh resonated in his chest. I remembered the person from that day. She seemed to have a sadness surrounding her. I pushed my legs up on the chair and climbed up on his lap. Once I found myself securely in his lap, I curled up until I was nestled, and his strong hand found its way to my head. We both needed to be comforted.

One cold night while I lounged in the great room, my legs stretched out next to the big opening with warmth coming from it. My soft belly got the brunt of the heat. Soft footsteps entered and Alisa plopped down next to me with her legs crossed in front of her.

"So, little one, how are you tonight?" She laughed when I cocked my head at her in curiosity. She smiled and rubbed my tummy.

Not wanting to be bothered, I stretched my body closer to the heat and warmth, wondering why she had decided to bother me.

"I am here to teach you what a female with powers *can* teach you. Something which, if I am right, is already inside you." She tickled me and I kicked a leg out. "From what I've heard, your witch will be a powerful one. You'll know the difference between different auras, and see the good and bad in people. I sense it's already inside you, by the way you are with Alexander and from what my father told me. Remember to *always* be there for those you care about."

After she stopped, I rolled over and asked, *you can understand me*?

"Yes. So could my father, though he didn't voice it. He could understand you, but wasn't able to talk in your head like Alexander. We're a very powerful troupe of gypsies. Though our magic isn't as strong as Alexander's, we do fine." She smiled.

Alisa pulled a round, shiny ball from her bag; an urge to sniff it overpowered me and I stretched my body and sat up on my haunches. I tilted my head at the odd object.

"This is a crystal ball," she explained while looking at my face. She placed the ball on some sort of silver base on the blue rug in front of her. "This will give us a glimpse into the life you are destined to live. But it must be our little secret, and trust me, it is important to know what will happen and what is in store for you. The more you are prepared for your life, the better you'll be able to protect her."

Instinct took over and I placed my paw gently on the ball. It felt cool, but the longer I kept my paw there the warmer it became. I cocked my head and looked at Alisa. In an instant, we saw a swirling mist of fog and two figures within the ball. The two females were different in appearance, but I sensed they had a bond similar to the one I had with Alexander, and it overwhelmed me. I couldn't make out their features, but I liked both of these human women already.

All of a sudden, the fog swirled and went hazy. The next scene showed a man with long brown hair as he held one of the women from the other scene. I didn't like him; the fierce urge to rip out his throat astounded me.

"Settle down, now. That is your witch's love. We're not sure about him yet." She waved her hand over the ball.

The aura that encased him kept changing from grey to a mixture of blue and purple to an array of different colors. Something about him gave me the impression he held evil inside him, but I became unsure every time his aura changed. I decided my job would be to keep an eye on this one.

something is among us

Present Time

The first time I encountered evil—or what Alisa later told me was evil—I had taken a walk around the grounds in the dark. I glanced up towards the sky and the round white ball shone brightly in the dark sky. In an instant the air around me changed from warm to chilly, the hair along my back rose quickly, and an eerie sensation rose in the darkness.

I stalked towards the bushes closer to the perimeter of the garden, curious and leery at the same time. My eyes scanned the pitch black of the gardens for what could be lurking. I saw a tall figure in a cloak move from the darkness into the light, a black hood covering its face.

"Ahh, you're a special one, aren't you?" As the voice spoke to me, the creature inched closer.

A loud growl came from deep within my chest; I pulled my lips back and showed off very sharp canines. The hair rose higher along my back, and I charged the figure cloaked in darkness.

A few feet from me, it knelt in front of me and put out its hand in an offer of peace. “It is all right, I won’t harm you.”

It seemed human, but something was off. This creature or human’s aura confused me. One minute it looked good and the next it swirled a different color. My head began to feel foggy. A high-pitched whine came from my throat, and I put my head down and rubbed it with my front paws.

I eased back on my haunches and watched while the figure slipped the hood back from its face. I stared at the pretty female, and her voice began to soothe me. I noticed something move along her body; it rippled when I tried to focus on it. As I stared I tried to place where I had seen such an animal. Then I remembered in the gardens, under the bushes, I had seen one slither on many occasions. This one slithered around her neck and hissed at me before it coiled around her arm.

“Hush, Asp,” she scolded the creature.

All of a sudden I heard Alisa’s voice call out to me. The soft crunching of her feet on the grass alerted me to her presence before I saw her.

She stood behind me and yelled, “Get out of here, evil one. Your kind is not wanted here.”

The stranger's evil laughter rang in my head, "I will, Alisa, but the dog and I *will* see each other again. However, she will not remember this meeting until the time is right." She laughed and disappeared in a puff of dark black and red smoke.

I ran to the spot where she had stood, barked loudly, and walked back towards Alisa. *She's gone now. Who is she*? I asked, bouncing around her feet while we walked, though I took extra care not to trip her on our way back to the castle.

"No one you need to concern yourself with, little one." She spoke in a worried tone. "I must let Alexander know about her, and the spell."

"Spell? What spell?" I asked, but she didn't answer me. I tried to dig into her mind but her thoughts were closed.

When we entered the house, she headed straight for Alexander and I headed to the kitchen to see Cook. She filled my bowl and patted my head before she went to the sink to finish her chores. The loud footsteps of the red one approached while I slurped up the last remnants of my meal, the bowl scratching on the floor while I tried to get every morsel. I looked up as he entered the kitchen, licking the remains of my meal from my lips.

"Little one, I hear you had a visitor." His voice contained much concern.

Yes, but I don't know who she was. I whined.

He picked me up and carried me toward the great room, where he sat down in the tan leathered sofa in front of the box where the warmth came from and looked me straight in the eyes. The flames danced in the reflection of his eyes.

"Well, it sounds like she knows who you are." He dug around in my head. "You must be careful when you meet her again. Though, because of the spell she placed on you, you will not remember meeting her tonight. Her future is foggy. Remember, a bigger evil is among us."

a special guest

After the visit from the mysterious stranger, my head began to clear but my memory of her had already begun to fade. I ran into Alexander's office for another day of training. Later, after a particularly good training day, we had a special guest come to visit us. I had retired to lounge in the front foyer, spread out lengthwise on my right side against the cold marble floor. A knock sounded on the door and I barely picked my head up from the coolness of the floor.

When the butler opened the door, a woman stormed into the castle in a whirlwind. The power stemming from her proved her to be very powerful. I had already learned much about auras, and I knew hers showed she had a kind and loyal heart. She wore very strange clothes, much different from what they wore in the castle. She demanded to talk to Alexander, and he came out of his office at the sound of the commotion.

"How may I help you, Madame Magnolia Delacroix?" he asked her in his thick Danish accent.

"My daughter is in trouble! I have foreseen her future, and an evil lurks and waits for the right time to strike. Though I fear my time here is at an end, I need to make sure her Guardian will be delivered on time. When she turns twenty seven I won't be with her any longer." She spoke very slowly, and with an accent which was unlike Alexander's or the others I had heard.

He strode over to the woman and placed a comforting hand on her shoulder.

"Calm down, madam, please," he pleaded with her.

"I will *not* calm down," she huffed emphatically. She turned to look at him. "And how do you know my name?"

Before he answered her, he waved to one of the servants. "Milly, would you bring us a tray of hot tea?" The servant curtsied and bustled out of the room towards the kitchen.

He continued once she seemed settled and a little calmer. "Ja, I have seen you and your daughter in a vision. We have been waiting for the time she turned of age and her Guardian would be needed."

After a few moments, I picked my head up off the floor and noticed the servant carried a large tray inside the room. It contained tiny cups and a pot with steam curling around from the top. The heavy tray almost made the tiny servant topple over, but she regained her composure, and with extra care placed it on a table in front of the woman and Alexander.

I stood up, stretched out my body, and padded in after her, and saw her curtsey when Alexander dismissed her. I sat down by the doorframe and watched the two left in the room with an inquisitive eye. He poured two cups of steaming tea and handed one to the woman.

The woman took it in her shaking hand, and Alexander cupped her hand around the tiny breakable cup. She looked up at him; her eyes brimmed with tears and one slipped down her cheek. He wiped at it with a cloth napkin. "It will be fine, Magnolia."

She nodded, and after she took a sip of her tea the woman looked around in amazement, and her gaze focused on the room. "May I see her?"

He turned around and directed her towards where I sat by the open doorway.

"Ah, is that her?" she asked with curiosity. I stood by the door, hesitant to enter.

"Yes. This little one is your daughter's Guardian, and I will deliver her to your daughter on her twenty-seventh birthday. Personally." He bowed his head in respect to her. "I have trained her well. She'll be ready to guard her with her life." He took a sip of his tea and placed it back on the little plate on the table.

The woman placed her cup back down on the tray and called me to her. I made a small move towards her and stopped.

"It is okay, girl," Alexander prodded me.

I walked over, sat down in front of her, and handed her my paw as my way of saying hello. She smelled of the sweetest smell ever, like flowers but a flower I'd never smelled before. I barked in response to her soft touch as she petted me. A flow of visions ebbed through my body at her gentle touch; I had witnessed my life through her. Either my powers had started to grow, or this woman had some heavy power.

I saw the witch I would soon be guarding, and I knew I would have a good life. It saddened me somewhat, because I knew I would be leaving Alexander soon, but he had been right...I would be a great Guardian. Sadness consumed this woman and I wondered why she hurt so badly.

"This one, Alexander, will be perfect for my daughter. She is divine. *Oh,* and her markings are extraordinary and unique." She picked me up and placed me in her lap, petting me while she picked up her cup and sipped her tea again.

"Yes she is, and in my vision it shows she will be tested, as will your daughter." The woman stared at him in a mixture of shock and awe. "Ja, but my dear Madame Magnolia, it is their destiny and fate, and will make them stronger together."

She placed her cup back down and looked me over more thoroughly this time. She tilted my head and checked out my paws.

"Sha t'bebe, my daughter will fall madly in love with you. And the city of New Orleans you will love; the spicy food, the sounds of the reverent jazz music...no fields to run through, but I will make sure you have a place of your own to play in." She ran her hand lightly over my ears. "And I am sure I can wrangle up some friends for you to play with." She winked at me and started to speak in a weird language.

Hear these words my vow to thee
My magic for you to always flow free
Should issues arise no need to fear
My magic will guide me forever near.
Two markings will be
But different when touched in the eve.

She touched me and a sudden electric current went through my entire body. "Just a little of my magic, to make sure. In case you ever become separated from my daughter, you will always be with her no matter what. Once you come in contact with her she will bear the mark...and so will you."

She stood up and thanked Alexander, placing something in his hand. He took it, glanced at it, and stuffed it in his pocket.

"Madame Magnolia, I know you've prepared for your absence from your daughter's life after you are gone. Please, know she will be in good hands with this little one."

She placed me back on the ground and wiped her face. "Thank you, Master Alexander...thank you." With that, she turned and left the castle.

my final goodbye...or is it

The day for me to leave the castle and head to my new home had arrived. The staff all came to wish me goodbye. Cook packed my favorite morsels in a bag and informed Alexander to give them to me on the flight.

"Goodbye. We shall miss you around this big empty place." She snuck me a secret piece of my favorite treat. I took it with care, gobbled it up, and licked her on the face. She leaned down, petted my head, and pulled a round item from her pocket.

"This, little one, is from someone special," she winked at me. "Your brother's family sent a special pink, leather collar to us for the day you would leave." She buckled it around my neck and smiled at me before she stood back up. The soft collar wrapped around my neck like an old friend.

Next to say goodbye was my new friend and Alexander's new scribe, Alisa. As she leaned down, water trickled from her eyes and dripped down her chin.

"My new little friend, I shall take care of Alexander and you will do fine in your new home." She patted my head and clasped a clear white, almost opaque, teardrop shaped stone to my collar.

"This amulet is a special gift from me and my father to you and your witch. Inside this precious stone is one single tear from your mother. On the day you were born, your mother dropped one single tear for each puppy to receive this special gift when they left."

I sat down and pushed the stone back and forth with my paw. It looked like the one my brother had. When I touched it, I caught a glimpse of a memory from my mother, and I could feel her presence around me. She showed me what happened after we were born. A single teardrop left her eye, pinged on the clear colored stones, and became encased in them forever.

Alisa interrupted my thoughts.

"My father would be proud of you." She sniffed and wiped her eyes with her fingers. Alexander came up beside her and handed her a piece of cloth, which she used to dab at the corners of her eyes. The precious gift hung from my new collar and I smiled up at Alisa, and mentally thanked her.

My mother, tall in stature, stood proud. *Like a mother should be*, I thought. I remembered my mother had chosen her life and to stay with Alexander, to protect him and serve him even though her witch had perished. It remained her duty to produce more Guardians and Warriors.

My daughter, you honor me with your patience and desire to be the perfect Guardian. It brings an abundance of pleasure to me that you will soon be with your witch. I know you will do great things. She nudged the amulet hanging around my neck. *In this symbol of my love I will always be with you...every day, like I have been with your brothers and sisters. You all have made Alexander and me proud, and one day I hope to see each of you again.* I nuzzled her and stepped back. I watched Alisa come up and stand beside my mother.

Once all the staff had wished me well on my new adventure and waved goodbye, Alexander picked me up and we left to travel to my new home and my new life. The trip to New Orleans, Louisiana proved to be a long one. For most of it, I rode on some sort of loud, metal box called a plane. Once we landed, Alexander, with all his magic, whisked us straight to my new home. I asked him why he didn't do the magic thing in the first place.

"Because no matter how much magic I have, the trip from Germany to Louisiana is a long one, little one." He smiled.

When we stopped on our whirlwind trip from the place that had the airplanes, we stood across the street from a giant sculpture of a man on a horse. I stared in awe at the towering sculpture in all its breathtaking beauty. The more we saw the more excited I became to have my new life start. We walked across the street and I saw some animals that reminded me of the ones at home. I squirmed in Alexander's hold to see these animals better.

"Those are mules to carry the tourists through this glorious city."

"Oh, I want to see them." I squirmed some more.

He walked towards them and let me sniff them on our way down the street. With me snuggled safely in his strong arms, we headed to my new home. I knew he held me tight and close to him because he would soon miss me. We had lived together for hundreds of years.

The city bustled with many people, and the loud noises were different than I had become accustomed to. The spicy aromas of food wafted through the streets, and I hoped my witch would lead me to where those aromas came from.

"I am sure she will, little one." He laughed and petted me. "But you must be hungry. Before I drop you off at your new home, let's find something quick to eat, Ja?"

He walked around the square and we saw a man selling long meat in fluffy bread to match.

Can we have one of those? I pleaded.

"Sure, little one." He walked up to the fat little man with no teeth and ordered two of the treats. I gobbled mine up with the gusto of a starved dog. The nice little fat man came over and gave me another one.

Alexander went to pay the man but he shook his head. From off in the distance I heard the noises of some sort of musical instrument. *What is that*? I asked.

"That is what they call a trombone, and your witch's mother spoke true; it is a most beautiful sound, called jazz."

What my witch's mother had told us came true with every step he took, closer to my new life filled with adventure, danger, but most of all love. He turned the corner and headed down the brick paved street. I knew we were close and my tail started to wag in anticipation of seeing my witch for the first time in person.

Alexander stopped in front of an iron gate. The creaky sound of the gate opening hurt my ears. We walked through a long tunnel and entered an open area hidden from the street. He placed me down on the ground while he searched for something.

I sat and waited anxiously, but then several see-through people flew toward me. They darted around me in swirling movements, and I decided to chase them. I tried to catch them but they flew higher out of my reach. I barked in protest at their unfair play.

"Ahem...now please don't rile the dog up before she meets her witch." He cleared his throat. The barely visible people nodded in his direction, then passed through me. They waved with mischievous smiles and hid back in the darkness of the cracks in the walls. I tried to follow, but they had disappeared. I barked loudly for them to come back, then bounded back over to Alexander. *What are they*? I asked him.

"Ahhh. They are what the humans call ghosts; they're souls who are lost or ones who don't want to pass on." He chuckled. "I presume those are the friends Madame Magnolia had been talking about when she visited the castle."

Resting on my haunches, I stared back toward the walls where the ghosts had gone and looked forward to playing with them again soon. He dragged a brown box out from beside the wall, picked me up, and placed me inside. The box was rough on my bottom as I sat there.

"Now be quiet, little one. She'll be out in a moment. I know you will soon have a name. One fitting for the Guardian you are to become. Named for your attributes, as your brother was." He winked at me.

He pulled a folded up note, with what looked like it had a hard substance on the back of it to seal the two edges together, from his pocket and stuck it inside the box with me. He reached down and petted me, and a soft whine came from me at the thought I would never see him again.

I wanted to bark at him I would miss him, but somehow I knew he knew this already. Our bond had always been strong, but he had begun to break it slowly and pulled his mind from mine.

"You must connect with your witch now."

Words hold strength this bond must break.
Power, love, and a destiny at stake.
By my side you shall be no more.
Hear the words, halt the inner war.
With another your fate is entwined.
With that soul you will soon bind.

With a final tug of his mind from mine the bond we had shared for so long was broken. My old life was ending and my new one had begun.

I licked his face one last time before he closed the lid. He left the tabs loose and walked away. I peeked the tip of my head out of the box to watch him walk around the corner. I knew he would wait to see the witch come out to find me. I stuck my head back down and curled up in a ball on the bottom of the box to wait for my new life to begin.

From inside the box I heard soft footsteps approaching the box. My head popped out of the box and I whined to get her attention. My witch, a special woman I was created to guard, headed down the steps towards me.

When she flipped back the flaps and peered in at me, I jumped out of the box full force. My instinct to bond with her overcame all of my senses. I had one thought; to lick and get close to her. She looked as she did in that magic ball of Alisa's, only better in person. Her aura turned a bright pink, and I knew instantly my life was complete. She tried her best to hold on to my body as it wiggled. Once I settled in her arms, she checked me out like her mother had. Her eyes fell upon the gift from my mother. At her touch, it flashed a myriad of colors. The moment the colors splayed an electric current hit us, and I knew we were officially bonded.

I wiggled in her arms again. She leaned down and grabbed the note, and smiled at me in her arms. "Let's go see where you came from and why you're in my courtyard."

She held me in her arms while we headed out of the gate Alexander and I had come through. Over the petite female's shoulder, the last thing I saw was Alexander hidden deep in the shadows. *My new life has begun, and it will be a fantastic one.* One destined to be great, or so they'd told me....

Turn the page for a sneak peek into Ghosts from the Past

CHAPTER ONE

A Friend or a Foe?

Present Day

My feet pounded the pavement as the urge to hide what I had become grew stronger with every step. What must she think of me, a hideous monster? Why had this happened to me? With the impulse to run until I could no longer move my legs, I moved with the utmost care, hiding out of sight of the human eye. It took me awhile, a few weeks, but I made it back home to the bayou.

For hours my worn and tired legs carried me to destination nowhere; the pain which I ignored started to settle and crawl up my calves to my thighs. Finally exhausted, I sat down beside a cypress knee that protruded from the ground, and my ass sunk deeper into the soft earth, close to the edge of the bayou. While I had a quiet moment, I contemplated how my life had turned out. It had been only a couple of weeks since I had first turned. I had a loving woman who had returned to my life, who I'd left because I was afraid to hurt her...and didn't want her to see the monster I'd become. Anger swelled inside me as I shook my head in dissatisfaction.

The memories flooded through again of us sitting at the table, my Rosie beside me, comforting me. The fateful day I found out how my life would change forever. I had forbidden Rosie to do anything to help me which would cause her pain. All because of this damn-it-to-hell curse.

It was not long ago I'd physically changed, my appearance being altered to one of a monster. The raw power that surged through me as I morphed into the wretched creature had me reeling almost instantly. And then the last night when I had seen Rosie and Athena heading down the street, I was angry and I wanted to hurt something. Before I could hurt her, thankfully, I recognized her. The look on her face when I saw it through the monster's eyes—my eyes—was a combination of fear followed by recognition. The witch's bright light emanated through the streets, shining down on my atrocious form, and I ran from the one person who would do anything she could for me. But the risk was too high.

The moment I left her side and ran down the alley my heart ached and I knew what had to be done. From around the corner, I hesitantly turned back in time to see a woman I somehow recognized. She was bent over, helping my beloved Rosie from the ground where she sat. The sadness floating from her to me broke my heart. Once I knew she was safe, I made up my mind to let her go. When I left her the next day, her scent was still heavily on me and her tears broke everything in my soul. I didn't know how either of us could come back from this. If I was broken, then I feared I had broken her spirit. This was not how it was supposed to be. So with the hardest decision I'd ever had to make behind me, I ran back home to the bayou.

The memories invaded and flooded my brain, as had all the memories of the past lately. Right now I had only received snippets of what seemed to be the past. And not only mine but those who'd shifted before me. The headaches were also getting more painful. Then memories of Rosie hit me again...the hurt in her eyes, the sound of her crying as her tears cascaded down her cheek. I had not been able to look back as she screamed out my name. My retreating figure could not bear to turn around. If I had, I would not have found it in me to leave. Her beauty continued to get to me. The onslaught of memories caused me to double over in pain. Massaging my temples, I tried my hardest to rid myself of the discomfort.

A sudden brisk noise pulled me from my thoughts. In the distance I saw a figure emerge from inside the ancient cypress tree high an oak ridge. I blinked at the person walking slowly towards me, then back at the tree. Had I really seen her come out of the tree? No. I could not have. I shook my head then closed my eyes.

When I reopened them, she was right in front me. I jumped back, shocked. “Geez, woman, you scared the shit out of me.”

She cackled. “Oh boy, I meant you no harm.”

I watched while her hair turned from black to white and back again right before my eyes. I rubbed my eyes with my knuckles, wondering if I had started to go crazy; after all, with what I had seen recently anything could happen. She looked at me with hollow sunken eyes. She reached out a long white boney hand to touch my shoulder. The moment her touch hit me I shivered, and not a good shiver.

She sat down on a stump and looked over at me. Her appearance changed before my eyes, from an old woman to a young one.

“Young man, what are you doing here? Don’t you have loved ones looking for you?”

I shook my head at her question. Anger bubbled to the surface, and I wondered why it was any of her business. I cocked a brow at her.

“The reason I am out here is none of your business; but if you must know, I left my girlfriend...all because she saw the real me. So I am out here,” I waved my hand, indicating the marsh and cypress trees of the bayou, “thinking maybe I should end it all. You see, I recently found out I am turning into a hideous monster, and I left the one person who I saw as the love...”

Before I could finish my statement she interrupted me. “Ah, you are a turning into a Rou ga Roux.” Her accent was hinted with subtle French.

Voodoo Vows

Voodoo Vows 1

The Guardians – A Voodoo Vows Tail

Bred by Magic

Coming Soon

Ghosts of the Past Voodoo Vows 1.5
Magical Memories-A Mother's Day short story
Gifted by Magic – The Guardians-
A Voodoo Vows Tail 2
Black Magic Betrayal- Voodoo Vows 2

About the Author

As a young girl, Diana Marie Dubois was an avid reader and was often found in the local public library. Now you find her working in her local library. Hailing from the culture filled state of Louisiana, just outside of New Orleans; her biggest inspiration has always been the infamous Anne Rice and her tales of Vampires. It was those very stories that inspired Diana to take hold of her dreams and begin writing. She is now working on her first series, Voodoo Vows.

Amazon Page: http://www.amazon.com/-/e/B00O97TWUO

Facebook:
https://www.facebook.com/diana.m.dubois

Goodreads
https://www.goodreads.com/author/show/7690662.Diana_Marie_DuBois

Instagram:
http://instagram.com/dianamariedubois

Pintererst:
http://www.pinterest.com/dianamdubois/

Twitter: https://twitter.com/DianaMDuBois

Tumblr: http://dianamariedubois.tumblr.com/

Website: www.dianamariedubois.com

47620445R00051

Made in the USA
Charleston, SC
14 October 2015